(Silk and Thorns #1)

by

L. K. RAYNE

And the heart that is soonest awake to the flowers is always the first to be touch'd by the thorns.

- Thomas Moore

Old Blooms

"They're dead."

The over-perfumed lady sniffed haughtily and pushed the vase of limp daffodils across the counter to me. She used both hands, the rings on each of her fingers skittering off the glass vase. Her small neck scarf almost fell off her shoulder before she snatched it in a huff like her day couldn't get any worse.

Technically, the daffodils were dead the moment they were cut` and wrapped in cellophane. I did my best impression of a charming smile, mentally pushing away a fantasy of me strangling her so that she'd hang limp like the flowers on the glass counter.

I could picture the tabloid blurb already: "Sierra Kinsey places movie producer's wife in chokehold in flower shop brawl."

"I see. When did you purchase these from us?" I asked pleasantly.

"I don't remember," she said, crossing her arms defensively over her Louis Vuitton bag. "Why does that matter?"

"Well it looks like you've had them for some time ma'am."

She furrowed her brows in righteous indignation. "So? What are you saying? That it's my fault they died?"

"No ma'am," I chose my words carefully, "We keep our flowers as fresh as we can, but the thing about cut flowers is—"

The lady shook her head and pointed her claw heatedly at April, who was currently taking shelter behind me. "Ask your employee, she was the one who sold me these dried flowers. How do you sleep at night?"

Just another day in the line of fire of someone perfectly primed to explode.

Right before closing too. Lovely.

"Just a moment please, ma'am." I excused myself and beckoned April to follow me into the back.

April gripped the outer layers of her dress. Her meticulously curled locks of hair tumbled around her shoulders as she swayed nervously. "I'm so sorry, Nev. I just—"

"Let me guess," I said, "she used up more than an hour of your time only to end up buying the cheapest bouquet we had out. And wait, I bet it was more than a week ago, based on the sorry state of those blooms."

April's eyes slid habitually to the right as her red lips pursed into the opposite direction. She always did that when she knew I was right.

"Either that or you," I made quotes in the air, "deliberately sold her some dried flowers when we have perfectly healthy ones all over the shop."

"Well, I guess it was more like two weeks ago," she mumbled.

"How long have we been in this together, Ms. Santos?"

She looked up at me, eyes glittering, eyelashes fluttering. "Since the beginning, since college, since forever, Nev!"

"Exactly. Why are you getting all apologetic when you know exactly how these stuck up lizard ladies are?"

"W-well you always let me take time off to run to auditions, and I'm so grateful to work here and be your employee, and I don't want to —"

"Oh my gosh," I threw my hands in the air, "tell me right away if I'm treating you like an *employee*!"

April took a deep breath to suppress her laughter. "Come on, Nev, the shop is growing and if I screwed things up…"

"You know by now that part of working at a boutique like this is dealing with the constant stream of entitled Mercedes driving ladies who think they're better than you because their jobs consist of going to pilates at 9AM prompt."

"Yeah! I know! Exactly! That's why I could've told her that...uh, cut flowers don't last forever after they bloom?"

I sighed. "April...sometimes the customer is wrong and doesn't want to admit it."

She looked down at her favorite cute red heels but I could see the little grin on her face.

"So what should we do?" April asked. She looked nervous watching me wring my hands together like I was imagining my fingers on someone's throat.

"Gotta grit our teeth and bear it in this case. Someone who doesn't understand that cut flowers have a relatively short display life is liable to get all her friends to trash us on Yelp. Not worth the headache."

April nodded. "You're right."

"We'll go back over there and pretend we're sorry and that this will never happen again. Do you think you can put those acting classes to use and look sad, like I chewed you out?"

April looked back up at me with the cutest sorriest puppy eyes I'd ever seen.

"Perfect."

When we made our way back to the front of the shop, April gave an award winning performance that greatly satisfied Mrs. Lizard and—after sealing the deal with a free bouquet—the lady was out the door and out of our hair. When April locked up the front door, the little bell made a satisfying jingle.

I cleared my throat loudly, turned up my nose and gave my best golf clap.

"Thank you, thank you!" April curtsied and clasped her hands together. "This is all so unexpected! I'd like to thank the Academy, my agent, my parents and most of all my best friend, Sierra. And, and, uh..."

I whirled my index finger in the air, signaling her to wrap up her speech.

"I really haven't taken that long!" April laughed.

I laughed too before motioning her to turn the sign hanging on the door to "closed" so we could get started on prep work for the Imperial Grand Hotel event tomorrow. April joined me in the back of the store as I got the ceramic vases. Since the event would be April's chance to take the lead, I let her play her favorite K-pop music videos in the background. Even though Thursdays were usually my day to pick the music, I conveniently forgot to mention it.

"So..." April began as I started arranging the vases in neat rows on the large work table.

I busily tugged at the baby's breath, untangling each branch from the bunch. "We went over this already, it's just another delivery," I said, hoping that she'd take the hint.

April pulled over a metal stool and started helping me with the flowers. She leveled a skeptical eyebrow at me. "Just another delivery? Sounds like someone is in," she sang the word, "denial!"

I continued working on the flowers without making eye contact. At this point, any reaction from me would only encourage her, and if I learned anything since we landed the Imperial gig, it was that April did *not* need any more encouragement when it came to the topic of Ethan Thorne.

She veiled the bottom of her face with a cluster of petite white blooms, then flashed me a dramatic look over the top, "I can picture it already. You're placing a fabulous bouquet on the table in the Crown Gallery—"

"Royal Ballroom," I corrected, "which is on the opposite side of—"

But April continued as if she hadn't heard me, "When you look up, he's entering the ballroom, tall, dark and oh so handsome in his tuxedo. You look away but you can't help yourself, so you shyly sneak another glance. And that's when it happens. Your eyes meet across the room, like a beam straight through the crowds of people. Your heart goes pitter-pat, pitter—"

"Pretty sure that pitter-pat will be from running around with a bunch of other vendors, since we're getting there a whole three hours before—"

"—electricity shoots up your spine and—"

I winced, "Sounds painful."

"—when he touches you, it's like not a single day has passed. Two souls, separated by the world, entwined by fate. Like two moths, fluttering," she crossed her hands at the wrists and flapped them, "unknowingly, dangerously, into the flames!"

She flapped frantically.

I couldn't help but crack up. Ever since I'd told her that I had once known Ethan when we were children, she'd been hounding me about our "reunion", describing one scenario after another. At the very least, each one was different, though recently I noticed that they were getting more and more outlandish.

April froze with her hands still forming moth wings, looking eagerly at me.

When I got control of myself, I said, "I'd rather not get burned in this wild fantasy of yours," then continued preparing the rest of the vases.

April let out a long sigh, deflated. She placed some loose stems down on the table. "Okay, fine...then how do you see this going down?"

"It doesn't," I said, placing roses into each thin vase, "We'll be long gone by the time the guests arrive. Real life doesn't work out like it does in your romance novels, you know."

"Hey, you read them too," she said.

"Uh, correction, I read *one*, and that was only because you begged me for two weeks straight."

April huffed and went to the other side of the room, where her polka-dotted red purse—perfectly matching her shoes—was hanging and retrieved her phone. She pecked at the screen for a few seconds, then held the phone up to me, confronting me with a full body shot of Ethan mid-walk like he was on his way to a meeting.

Was he really that handsome? The baby fat on the face that I remembered had melted away into a chiseled jawline, framed by a neatly trimmed beard. His gaze gave the impression of stoic seriousness like he was someone who floated above the concerns of mere mortals.

I purposefully made eye contact with April and then shrugged.

April turned her phone back to herself and started scrolling. "Ethan Thorne, possibly the most eligible bachelor of the century, is defying odds with the most ambitious engineering project since the launch of the space shuttle."

"It's just some fluff piece for that high tech transportation system, I'm sure they're exaggerating."

"You know about it!" April squealed excitedly.

"Who wouldn't? The news can't get enough of it."

I avoided googling him nowadays, but after that humid summer fifteen years ago, I'd occasionally looked him up, curious about how he had turned out. With how high profile his family was, it wasn't hard to find out what he was up to. He graduated as valedictorian of his Stanford University class before starting an engineering firm making biomedical devices. Then he sold that company before doing the same with a few more companies. Then came the bidding to build some sort of fancy transportation system, the first of its kind between Los Angeles and San Francisco.

Now I couldn't help but hear his name in the news all the damn time.

"Tell me he doesn't look like he stepped out of a GQ cover," April demanded.

He actually had been on the cover of a GQ magazine a few months ago, but I wasn't about to feed this monster.

I rolled my eyes then started to set the prepared vases into the milk crates on the floor. "I can admit that he's attractive, but just because we chased each other through the woods for a couple of weeks when we were kids, doesn't mean we're fated to be together."

"Fated to be together," April murmured to herself.

"It's just a saying."

April raised an eyebrow at me.

"Come on, don't get all mystical on me, you know I don't believe in that stuff."

Her eyes scanned me up and down skeptically, like it was only a matter of time.

"Anyway," I continued, "I'm sure Ethan's a busy guy. Doesn't make sense to get in the way even if we did see him."

April looked at me appalled. "How can you not even *wonder* if there's something there?"

I pinched my thumb and forefinger together. "You might be projecting a teensy bit," I said. "Could it be that *you're* the one who can't get him off your mind?"

She considered it for a moment. "Are you saying that you'll catch a cold tomorrow and then I'll be solely responsible for setting up? Leaving me to...interview the billionaire?"

"Fat chance," I snorted. Then I tapped a finger pensively on my chin, "Maybe I shouldn't let you take lead now that I know you're planning an impromptu interview with the guest of honor."

"You've been prepping me for the past three months. I got this!" She flicked her hair over her shoulder. "And don't worry, you can count on me. Watch and learn..."

The mischievous grin she flashed me wasn't comforting. April, noting my skepticism, crossed her legs, produced a pen and held it to her smartphone like she was a hard hitting journalist. "So, *Mr. Thorne*...to what do you owe your success?"

"See! That's what I mean!"

"I'm kidding, Nev," April said, giggling. "Sisters before misters. I am *not* going to mess up this delivery for the shop, even if it means I'll miss out on a once in a lifetime chance to find out what a bad boy billionaire is *really* like...in bed." She giggled again at her own joke.

She swiped through some more photos on her phone, then presented me with another one, this time a half-body shot. Ethan was dressed in a white suit exiting a Ferrari, his body elegant and graceful despite the stillness of the photo. That same serious expression. "Mmmm," April sighed. "I bet a man like that knows his way around a pair of cuffs."

"Ho-okay," I said, "you've officially gone off the deep end. I'm pretty sure Ethan isn't like that."

"How do you know?" April challenged, swiping through more pictures on her phone. "You said yourself you haven't spoken to him in fifteen years. I mean, look at those eyes." She placed her phone on the table next to me displaying a headshot so that I could get a good look while she finished organizing the vases.

I had certainly changed over the years, and now, looking at the photo April was showing me, I wondered how much Ethan had changed too. Was there still anything of the dorky kid hiding behind the suave exterior? I wasn't going to let it slip to April that I was a tiny bit interested. I mean, I wouldn't have turned down a chance to catch up with him to find out what kind of man he'd become… If only to satisfy my curiosity.

My eyes lingered on the photo. It was hard for me to reconcile this new version of him with the bookish boy that I once knew. His eyes were the same dark shade, but though the corners of his eyes crinkled into a relaxed smile, now there was a glint of something else under the surface. Dark and intense. Maybe April was right, maybe Ethan was exactly the type of dangerous playboy that he seemed to be presenting to the media.

But unlike April, I wasn't prone to flights of fancy. I understood the chances of us meeting at the event tomorrow was nil. And given how that summer way back then had ended, I doubted that he ever wanted to see me again.

I mentally shook away those unpleasant memories. "April, that picture definitely looks edited. Way too dramatic."

April leaned over to take another look at the picture while holding one of the crates. She tilted her head, considering, before flicking her eyes back at me. "You sure you aren't projecting a teensy bit?"

"Very funny. Come on, that's the last crate, let's head home."

"Don't be scared Nev, sometimes the universe conspires —"

"If the universe was really conspiring to fulfill my deepest, darkest, fantasies, I'd have a slice of Death by Chocolate cake in front of me right now."

She rolled her eyes. "The universe gives us what we need, *not* what we want."

I let April have the last say on the topic. We'd have a full day tomorrow, and I didn't want to get her riled up about "the universe" when she had plenty on her plate already.

After we closed up, I dropped April off at the apartment she shared with Roger and Philippe, a stunt couple she'd met through a film production, and finally headed home.

Tomorrow would be like every other event: quick, simple, and easy.

Big Cats

April tapped her freshly manicured fingernails along the rim of the steering wheel, her work gloves sitting partially tucked into the front pocket of her work apron. "Marigold Sunshine" was the nail polish color, as she had cheerfully announced upon bouncing into the shop for her shift yesterday. For every major event we did, she always painted on a new nail color. Today's color matched the pale yellow dress that peeked out from under her work apron.

When we first started doing deliveries, I kept warning April that she'd chip her nails since our jobs always included some manual labor, but she somehow knew how to keep them looking perfect. For whatever reason, I could never keep mine looking professionally done. It might have had something to do with my weekend trips to the indoor rock climbing wall or plain old carelessness, but either way, I certainly wasn't going to chance it even if we did wear gloves.

April was focused on the busy highway as we made our way to the Imperial Grand Hotel. Their gorgeous ballroom with a breathtaking view of the city was an exciting location, even if we'd be spending most of our time behind the scenes. We were making pretty good timing despite the usual bumper to bumper Los Angeles traffic.

"I can hear your voice in my head, Nev."

I realized that I'd been staring at her. "What do you mean?"

"You know I'm ready for this, but you look like you're about to pester me about something."

"I wasn't. Your nails look nice."

"Nev."

"What? They do!"

"Nev."

I sighed heavily. April always knew when I was a tad nervous for her despite her seemingly perpetual confidence. "Well, I wasn't going to make a fuss *yet* anyways. This is your first time taking point after all. I want to make sure you don't get overwhelmed."

"I'm ready for this! You won't need to do a thing. I'm great at delivering, and setting up, and presentation, and—"

"Not so great at networking."

She gripped the steering wheel and flashed me a shocked look. "What? I am *so* good at that!"

"Chitchatting, yes. Networking…"

"But it's the same thing!"

"We need to make connections, April, not flirt with the staff."

"I do not flirt with them! It's called having a nice conversation," she said the words cheerily.

"You can't only have 'nice conversation' with only the nice looking young men, you know?"

"I don't do that on purpose!"

That was true. April had a natural bubbliness; a type of charm that was hard for guys to ignore. It helped her chat up whoever we were working with, but it made it difficult for her to connect with the ones that mattered. I started in again on my usual talk, "If we can get friendly with the right people, they'll—"

"—refer business to us, I know, I know," April finished, tired of hearing the refrain so often.

I dropped the topic, tired of it myself.

After a few moments of silence, April shot me a sly grin. "Is that what you were doing with Mr. Cute Photographer at the wedding last weekend? 'Getting friendly?'"

I stared straight ahead at the tops of the cars on the busy highway. "He gave me his business card so it was purely a professional exchange."

"A number scribbled on a napkin is so *not* a business card," she said.

I shook my head, trying not to smile. There wasn't anyone to blame but myself for walking into that one. It was true. William, or "Billy" as he insisted I call him, seemed more interested in me than our flower shop, but enjoying the attention, I had taken his "business card" anyway.

"I had to be quick before he set his eyes on you," I teased, thinking on my feet. April was usually the one that got all the male attention, so it was refreshing, and honestly exciting, to get a bit for myself.

"We'll see when we get there," she said cryptically before putting her full attention back on the road. It looked like she had more to say so I waited, but she remained silent, despite the suspicious smile ghosting the corner of her lips.

Even though I'd never admit it to her, all those hypothetical run ins with Ethan Thorne had wormed their way into my brain. I knew the impossibility of meeting him today. Never mind the logistics, it would be highly unprofessional for a vendor to accost a distinguished guest, especially since the chances of him remembering me were slim to none.

Nevertheless, I had spent the previous night slipping into one fever dream after another. They were too hazy to remember, but from the recurring motifs of Ethan Thorne's ruggedly handsome face, a field of baby's breath, and ragged panting, the theme was clear enough. If my subconscious was sending me a message, as April might say, then it was my duty to make sure that my subconscious did not get its way, universe be damned.

Not wanting to be accused of thinking too loudly again, I looked out my window at the exit lane which was backed up almost half a mile. At least our lane was still moving even if it'd be another five miles until we got to our exit. Hopefully it wouldn't look like a bottle neck. We were lucky to have loaded the van and left the shop early enough that there was plenty of time budgeted for the setup once we arrived at the Imperial.

I was careful to build in ample wiggle room with our delivery schedule so that April wouldn't feel too rushed handling her first time leading. Hence, the early start. The plan was to get in, do our job—that is, let April do her job with me standing around as backup—then get out. No Ethan involved, and definitely no interviews.

In fact, April hadn't mentioned a single thing about her favorite billionaire today which was starting to make me feel nervous. After her prolonged silence, I could almost feel a spot burning into the back of my head as if she had lasers coming out of her eyes.

There it was. The April I somehow loved and adored. I knew she wouldn't be able to drop it.

"Alright," I said turning to look at her, "now I can hear *your* voice in my head."

She continued looking at the cars ahead innocently. "I didn't say anything."

"Just because I've resorted to chatting up wedding photographers at events doesn't mean that Ethan Thorne is the solution to my dry spell."

Instead of responding, April giggled while I sulked.

"Well?" I asked, "Isn't that exactly what you were going to say?"

"I was going to say that you don't give yourself enough credit," she looked at me genuinely, "I think it's cool how you get out there and reel the guys in. But how *curious* that you were the one who brought up Ethan today. I think we both know what's on your mind." She arched an eyebrow expertly, the look she'd been practicing since our college days.

"Hey, some of us have to work harder than others at getting dates, and the only reason Ethan's on my mind is because you wouldn't stop talking about him for weeks."

"Nuh-uh!" she whined childishly.

I chuckled at how silly she sounded. "And you're making me sound like some kind of predator."

"Maybe you are. Maybe you haven't met the right one yet because all the boys you meet are house cats, and you're a jungle cat." April made a Marigold Sunshine tipped claw at me and hissed.

"Please don't tell me you're on another shapeshifter romance binge," I said. "Because last time, you had to profile every guy we came across by his spirit animal."

She grinned. "And I got pretty good at it too, don't you think? What's Ethan?"

"I don't know, a penguin? Because he wears a lot of suits?"

"Penguins waddle. Does he strike you as the kind of man who has 'waddle' in his repertoire?"

My silence was answer enough for April.

"Mmhmm, nope. He saunters. Slides. Stalks."

"Um... John Travolta in Grease?" I offered.

April let a burst of laughter slip. "John Travolta isn't an animal! Ethan's totally cool. Controlled. In charge. A predator, like you." She lowered her voice to a dramatic whisper. "A panther."

I tried hard not to roll my eyes. "What, so we're both big cats now?"

I didn't have to search far to see where April had come up with that idea. The flyer for the event laying on the dashboard said that the Conservation Fund was collecting donations for their new Big Cat Wildlife Preserve project.

"That's right, and you and I both know what happens when a tasty morsel is dangled in front of a cat."

"You get cat scratch fever?"

"Nooo!" April protested with her whiny voice. After a moment she looked at me sideways, "But you'll get an entirely different kind of fever alright...wink wink nudge nudge."

"I think you're supposed to do the wink and nudge, not say them."

Our laughter almost drowned out the little beeping chirp coming from April's apron pocket.

"That might be Giselle," April said, suddenly focused, "Can you check it for me?"

I reached inside April's apron pocket and unlocked her phone.

OMG ARE YOU HERE YET?

I felt the hairs on the back of my neck stand. It was indeed a text from Giselle Dubois, who was in charge of running the event for the Conservation Fund. We'd become close from my days as an event manager, and nowadays, she still counted on us for flowers. I knew her well enough to know that all caps meant something serious.

No, be there in 20-30

The return text was immediate.

GOOD. TAKE SOUTH ENTRANCE.

I wanted to ask her why because the north entrance was closer, but she read my mind.

PIPE BURST. MOVING TO BANQUET CENTER.

"What is it? What is it?" April asked, bouncing in her seat. "Uh oh, you're so quiet, it must be bad. Is it Giselle?"

"Yeah, pipe burst."

"What!?" April almost shrieked. "Oh no, poor Giselle! Does this mean I don't have to network for business cards?"

I gave her a disapproving look.

"Okay, okay! Sheesh, just trying to lighten the mood!"

Friendly Help

The loading dock of the Imperial Grand Hotel was packed with vans, cargo trucks, and a number of golf carts jammed in wherever there was room. From my past life as an event manager, I could tell immediately that setup was going to run overtime. At this rate, the vendors wouldn't even be able to get all their equipment into the hotel, much less set up in an entirely new room.

I ran through my mental checklist of damage control as I leaned forward in the passenger seat to get a better view. April pulled in as far as she could, lining up our van behind the other new arrivals. I sucked in a breath of air. "Giselle will need to prioritize moving the larger trucks out of the loading area first so that smaller vehicles can stagger themselves in the—"

"I can't see her from here," April interrupted.

I could only hear her voice dimly as I continued to scan the scene, making quick calculations in my head.

April craned her neck to try to see past the chaos. "Didn't she say she would meet us in the loading area?"

"She'll have to assign a couple of staff to shunt traffic to the secondary loading dock," I muttered to myself, "lined up right here to make room for those exiting so that—"

"Don't get too excited about this mess, you weirdo." April gave me a side eye.

"I'm just excited we're finally here," I said offhandedly, more so to convince myself than anything.

"Uh-huh, there's a difference between mild excitement and freakish exhilaration."

April was right, I was wrapped up in some sort of weird trance state. I hadn't realized how much I missed the adrenaline rush of pulling together an event at the last minute.

I spotted a tall woman wearing a dark pantsuit weaving a golf cart in between the parked trucks.

"There she is!" I yelled. I unbuckled my seatbelt and whipped it off so fast that the metal could have left a dent in the door. I was almost halfway out of the van before I caught myself. Turning back toward April, I said, "Wait, wait. I did promise to back you up."

She flashed me a knowing look.

"Oh my gosh, get out there and help her already!" she said, trying not to laugh.

"Are you sure?" I asked, putting a hand on my knee to stop it from bouncing up and down.

"C'mon, Nev. I know how much you miss the chaos. Besides, Giselle needs you way more right now and if the event's a disaster, who cares if the flowers are pretty? As the lead on this job, I order you to go help her!" April made an exaggerated shooing motion. "Out out out!"

"Okay, I'll be back as soon as I can," I said, then jumped out of the van and headed toward the loading dock on foot.

Giselle spotted me, parked the golf cart, then waved at me to hurry. I scurried over and slid in beside her. "Oh, Sierra!" she said, giving me a quick hug.

Her back was cold and wet. When I pulled away, I gestured my wet palm at her. "Oh no, did you?"

"Ugh, yes! I had to move everyone directly impacted by that stoo-pid pipe!" Her French accent always slipped out when she was stressed. "I am so very glad to see you." A big grin slid across her face. "And early too!"

"How can I help?"

Giselle's eyes softened with relief. "I knew you'd ask."

Wet Silk

The next couple of hours flashed by in a blur as Giselle and I wrangled the vendors and their equipment into the smaller area of the Banquet Center, printed out new signs directing the guests, and put out various other last minute fires. Giselle and I had worked closely so often in the past that it was easy for me to slip into the old role.

By the time we were finished, I was glad that I'd chosen to wear my comfortable pair of black flats. Giselle took it from there while I returned to the loading area to look for April. Hopefully she was doing okay by herself.

I saw our van up ahead with the big yellow sunflower on the side and hustled over quickly. I heard April's voice coming from the back of the van and slowed down. She obviously had company.

"No no, thank you," April said in a perky tone. "Like I said before, I really don't need any help."

I caught sight of April first. She had tied her hair in a half-ponytail so it wouldn't get in her way but her bottom curls were still bouncing playfully around her shoulders.

When I got closer I saw a lanky young man with a buzzcut leaning against our van. He was wearing the formal white attire of one of the wait staff, so he should've been inside setting up for the guests, but what really got me was that one of his grubby hands was propped up on our van door.

"But what if you dirty your lovely dress?" the young man said, raising his eyebrow in what he imagined was a sexy expression.

Clearly, April's hints that she wasn't interested had gone way over his head. Not only was he slacking off when he should've been doing his job, but he was also preventing April from doing hers. Irritation rose in my chest but I deliberately slowed my step so I wouldn't end up tackling him. Giselle probably wanted all of her wait staff uninjured, especially with everything going on.

"I'm used to working in dresses," April replied politely.

"I bet they all look great on you with those legs," he said.

April, still polite, said, "I'm sorry, I really do need to finish setting these up."

"Oh of course, here," he insisted, "let me help."

The last thing we needed tonight were some inexperienced hands handling our vases. I took a deep breath so that I wouldn't end up doing something I would regret, and stood there for a moment, unnoticed by the two of them, before I couldn't take it anymore.

I stepped out suddenly right between the guy and April. "Didn't you hear her?" I asked.

He turned to me in shock, clearly flustered by my sudden appearance, "Uh—"

"Get out of here, kid," I jerked my thumb over my shoulder, "The guests will be arriving any second."

April shot me an amused look, surprised but pleased that I was back.

The guy blubbered, looking to her for support. She studied her Marigold Sunshine nails, suddenly finding them fascinating.

I took another step toward the waiter. He looked like the type that would need clear instructions, possibly paired with a threat. "I'm sure Giselle would be interested in learning which of the wait staff missed the all hands meeting...*Todd*," I said, looking pointedly at his name tag. "Now scram."

The guy blanched and scuttled away without another look back.

"He would've gone away eventually," April said with a sigh, "but I appreciate it Nev. Thanks. I can't believe you called him 'kid.'" She chuckled.

"Come on," I said, "I'll help you wrap up."

But there were only two lonely crates left in the back of the van.

"Looks like you didn't need me at all!" I said, admiring her handiwork. "You're a beast!"

April let out a hooting laugh. "Better believe it! This girl is on fire!"

I laughed too, relieved to see that April was having a good time despite the stressful situation. While we took the service elevator up to the hall leading to the Banquet Center, April updated me on her progress with setup and I told her how things had gone with Giselle. We were both in a pretty good mood since the event was now back on track and I felt way better knowing that April had her end under control.

I set the crates down in the corner and started to unpack the vases from the protective straw. At the opposite corner of the room, we could see a few early guests starting to filter in, but it wasn't a big deal considering the pipe disaster had been taken care of. Ideally, we would've been done with the flowers and out of there by now, but given what Giselle and I had to work with, I was pretty happy with how things had turned out.

The casino tables were organized neatly, with the dealers ready to entertain the guests. Cocktail tables were scattered in between the casino games for the guests to stand around and mingle. The open bar was ready to go at the end of the room, and most of the floral arrangements were tastefully placed, despite the layout changes, courtesy of April.

"Alright, so where do you want these, Ms. Santos?" I teased.

April had a vase tucked in each elbow, both arms full. She tilted her head to the center table, "Large one there," she swung her head to the right, "and the small one there."

April went to place her vases in the far corner of the room where there were a pair of matching tables.

I set the small arrangement down on the corner table, then went to put the larger one on the center table. Once I placed the coral-themed arrangement down, I fussed with a few of the green hypericum berries that were a little too tightly bunched.

When I leaned back to inspect the overall arrangement, there, across the room, were a pair of dark intense eyes staring directly at me.

I ducked behind the flowers, a clench of panic gripping my heart.

Those eyes could not have belonged to anyone else but Ethan Thorne.

I could hear April's soft voice in my head singing, *"You look away but you can't help yourself so you shyly sneak another glance...and that's when it happens."*

Eyes meeting from across the room as I put the flowers down? You had to be joking. April just made that up. The last minute scramble must've exhausted me and set my imagination working overdrive, making me see things that weren't there.

I slowly exhaled and straightened, pretending like I was still studying the flower arrangement, but I couldn't help a more purposeful glance past the bouquet. My eyes locked on the other end of the room.

Well, I hadn't been mistaken about one thing.

Ethan Thorne had arrived.

He stood greeting the small throng of people who had gathered around him, shaking hands with a soft smile. The hairs on the back of my neck were still standing, but Ethan hadn't made eye contact earlier. He had been looking around the room the same way politicians did, making sure everyone felt seen.

Secure in the knowledge that he hadn't spotted me, I stopped sneaking glances and studied him openly. So many years had passed that he never would've recognized me anyway.

Ethan Thorne was dressed in a very dark navy tux. People either paid out of their nose to look that good or had the magical fashion touch like April. As I watched him work the room, I tried to pinpoint what it was that made him so entrancing to watch. Finally, as the crowd around him dispersed, I figured it out.

In the weeks leading up to the event, I'd seen my fair share of pictures of Ethan, but none of the still images had been able to capture the grace of his movement. Seeing it in person was a sight to behold. Power, barely restrained by taut control.

He'd come a long way from the gangly, scrawny kid I remembered. But honestly, what did I expect?

Sometimes hormones could chisel a god out of a man.

With a start, I realized that while I'd been ogling him, trying to picture the firm muscles flexing beneath his tux, Ethan Thorne had started walking toward my direction.

Okay, Sierra. You got a good satisfying look, time to hightail it outta here before he sees you.

No reason to tempt fate.

Even though things hadn't played out like April predicted, her fantasies still had me spooked. I stepped out from behind the flowers, careful to avoid tracking Ethan in my peripheral vision. It's like they tell you when you're learning how to drive, don't stare into the oncoming headlights, or you'll end up drifting across the double yellow lines.

I turned my attention to searching for April. She wasn't at the tables across the room where I'd seen her last. Had she circled around to the other side of the hall while I was too busy gawking at Ethan? I checked the other side of the hall, every table already had flowers on them, but April was nowhere to be found. Where the hell was she?

I heard her footsteps on my right.

"April," I said, turning...

...to see dark, intelligent eyes, capturing me in their gaze.

That was definitely not April.

Ethan Thorne was nearly on top of me and he was still approaching, his shoulders shifting smoothly like he was stalking prey.

His eyes never once moved from my face. It had been a false alarm earlier, but this time he definitely saw me.

He *saw* me.

My mind stuttered like an old movie running out of film. No way. No way, no how. This wasn't happening.

Go now, Sierra! MOVE IT!

But my body was paralyzed, pinned to the spot.

My breath caught in my throat. My head swam. Heat ached between my thighs like I was drowning in a pool of liquid sex. I could hear my blood pounding through my ears in rhythm with April's sing-song words, "your heart goes pitter-pat." Though faintly, I noted that this wasn't a romantic sort of pitter-pat, more of a "I'm going to need an ambulance after I pass out and hit my head on the marble floor pitter-pat."

Ethan stared at me, an inscrutable expression on his face as he circled around the cocktail table, closing the rapidly decreasing distance between us.

The room lurched sideways for a dizzying moment and I stumbled backward. In a blind panic, I reached out and grabbed a fistful of tablecloth, taking the cloth and the vase and the flowers down with me.

Stale flower water streaked across Ethan Thorne's freshly creased pants.

The vase smashed on the floor, scattering into a million pieces as the flowers jounced lightly, before coming to a limp rest.

A hush fell over the room, a sharp contrast to the ringing echoes of ceramic crashing against marble.

Ethan took a single step back and frowned.

I was in deep shit.

Heat rose to my cheeks and I averted my eyes downward. It was way too embarrassing to keep gazing into his face while an entire room full of people watched the fiasco unfold in front of them like it was the evening's main entertainment.

A dark wet spot spread through the fabric of his pants. From the look of the fine Italian threads, his pants looked like they cost more than the flower shop pulled in, in a month. A good month.

I replayed the moment over and over in my head like a broken tape, wishing I could rewind time.

"I'm so so sorry, sir," I finally managed to stammer, "would you like a towel?"

Ethan stared at the folded white towel I'd produced from my work apron as if he'd never seen such an alien artifact. No anger. No histrionics. Given how wet his pants were, he was acting surprisingly reserved. Or maybe he was seething in rage, waiting for the right moment to blacklist our flower shop in front of all the guests.

"Um, it's here if you need it." I said, quickly setting it on top of the table for him. I ducked to the floor so I wouldn't have to keep looking at him.

Thankfully, as soon as I crouched down, the rest of the room returned to its previous murmur. They must've moved on to something more interesting. Either that, or they felt that enough time had passed to start discussing it amongst themselves. Speaking of time, where the hell was April anyway?

On my hands and knees, I searched for the shattered pieces of the broken vase, while moving the flowers to one side. I stacked the larger pieces of ceramic, lifting the side of the tablecloth, now hanging almost all the way to the floor, to check for stray shards underneath.

For a brief moment, I considered crawling underneath the tablecloth and hiding until everyone in the room disappeared. But before I could embarrass myself even further, Ethan bent down on one knee next to me, until his face was just above my head.

I tried my best to ignore his proximity and redoubled my efforts to clean up.

Ethan leaned in, making me feel as if there was a strange intimacy between us, as if we were the only children in a room full of adults, playing our own secret game.

A memory came then, unbidden. The two of us, by the lake shore, crouching next to an ant hill, a skinny twig in Ethan's hand.

Do you think ants ever leave their colony? For good?

Maybe if you keep poking them. Give me that stick already.

Why did I always think of the dumbest stuff whenever I was nervous?

I had picked up almost all the pieces of broken vase when I noticed the crimson ribbon on the floor next to Ethan's knee. It had been tied around the arrangement in a decorative bow, but now lay in a sad puddle of water. Had April tied this particular bow yesterday, or had I? They all looked the same to me.

I reached for the silk ribbon, but Ethan snatched it first. I immediately withdrew, careful to avoid any sort of physical contact. He caressed the silk between his slender fingers as if he was memorizing the feel of it.

"Thank you so much," I said, my palm outstretched, feeling peevish that I was afraid to even touch him. "I can take that for you."

Ethan's eyes glittered and he pulled his hand back quickly — almost possessively — tightening his fist around the ribbon.

A voice came from above us. "Damn it, you are *not* getting out of this, Ethan. Come on, we need to take care of those pants."

Ethan rose, finally breaking the connection between us.

I craned my neck up. The voice had come from a stunning blonde woman, about my age, wearing a charcoal sheath dress. The blonde woman's black ankle strap heels clacked purposefully as she led Ethan away.

April appeared suddenly by my side and I almost fell on my butt. Not seeming to notice this, she started helping me pick up the stacked pieces of the unfortunate vase, putting them into one of our crates after removing an equivalent backup vase for the table.

Great timing, barely a moment too late to save me.

"Oh. My. God..." she sang, "The universe is sending you a message!"

"April..." I said through clenched teeth.

She smiled happily, her eyelashes batting at me. "Mmhm?"

I let out a long breath as I watched Ethan and the blonde woman disappear around the corner. "Did you even *see* what just happened?"

In The Cards

"Got any Jacks?" April asked. She leaned over, pretending to peek at my cards.

I didn't bother covering my hand from April's obvious attempt to cheat and mumbled a "nope, go fish," rather unenthusiastically.

The utility stairwell echoed softly, the rumblings of the remaining vendors contained to the area beyond the exit doors. The stairs were tucked away, behind the staff areas, hidden from the hotel guests.

The two of us were sitting on one of the steps leading up to the next floor. We included breakdown at this event, and planned to wait for the event to be over before collecting and taking away the flowers the hotel didn't want to keep. There wasn't any harm in indulging in April's fun in the meantime.

April, humming an upbeat tune, drew another card from the deck sitting between us and added it into her hand. She was probably hoping her cheerful disposition would rub off on me with enough exposure.

"I know exactly what you're doing, April."

"What do you mean?" She gave me an innocent look, but I could see past that charade.

Accidents were par the course for a busy setup, but I was so stupid to draw Ethan's attention. Now, not only were the chances of him recognizing me higher, but instead of perhaps bumping into each other normally, the "universe" had to go and let *that* happen. My cheeks felt hot thinking about that embarrassing exchange. I wanted to forget that it happened and never see Ethan again. Ever.

"You're trying to distract me from the fact that I completely humiliated myself, not just in front of the one important man out there tonight, but another fifty of L.A.'s most ritzy."

"Aww, I'm pretty sure it wasn't fifty." April opened her arms to me, not realizing she was simultaneously revealing her cards. "Hug?"

I sighed.

April went in for the hug anyway. Her petite arms somehow always managed to feel warm and engulfing.

I leaned into April and sighed again, wishing to drown in her comfort. "I'm going to find a time machine and jump forward a hundred years into the future until everyone who witnessed that is dead."

April pulled back and made her signature puppy eyes at me. "But, what about me?"

"You can come with. Ethan though...definitely not."

"Well, you can't really blame him for what happened."

I shrugged, then huffed. "Let him grow old and wrinkled. What kind of cruel universe turns a little scrawny kid I used to play tag with into some kind of Greek god?"

"Girl, you got a strange definition of cruel..." She was dishing out a side-eye, and I could see a small smirk curled at the corner of her mouth.

"What else would you call it? And don't start with me on fate."

April busied herself by reorganizing her cards, accepting that I just wanted to vent and wallow in my misery. I couldn't help feeling a little guilty for being a sourpuss.

"Got any fours in there?" I asked hopefully.

"Nope, go fish."

I drew another card.

"You have to admit though," April started, letting a mischievous smile spread across her face before continuing, "it makes for a pretty good meet cute." Her eyebrows jumped suggestively.

"Okay, now you've got a strange definition of cute. Puppies are cute. Kittens are cute. Even baby possums are cute. But what happened out there was not cute," I said, shuddering. "More like downright cringey."

"When it's happening to you, it probably feels that way, but hey, you know...'the cringier the meet, the hotter the sex.'"

"No one has ever said that. Besides sex is the last thing I want from him."

"Mmhm…" April peeked over her cards. "Got an ace?"

I searched my hand.

"Well, what do you want from him?" April asked.

I handed the ace of hearts over. "Never to see him again."

April took the ace and seemed to ponder this. After a moment her eyes went wide. "You are so right," she said, punctuating each word.

I nodded, satisfied that April and I were finally on the same page. "Mmhm," I mirrored her usual tone.

"I would have never come up with that plan."

"What?"

"Ethan isn't some regular guy you can pick up at a bar. He's a titan of industry with loads of sexy socialites throwing themselves at him."

I crossed my arms. "What does that have to do with—"

April smushed her index finger against my mouth. "Sierra, you are a bona fide genius. What's more enticing to a man like that than a real challenge?" She swiped her hand like a claw and made a strangely accurate meow. "Kitty needs to hunt."

Of course April would think that.

"Well, that is *definitely* not my plan, but you're welcome to give it a shot if you like," I said.

April shook her head. "There is no way I'm standing between the universe and its goal. This is Ethan and your story."

I rolled my eyes. "Spilling some water on his pants doesn't mean that there's going to be a heartwarming reunion story. Besides, I bet you Ethan doesn't even remember that I exist."

April suddenly grabbed my hand and pumped it up and down, face lit up like a Christmas tree. "I'll take that bet! Loser pays for Korean Barbeque."

I looked at her funny. Was this another way to try and make me feel better?

"Why leave all the fun for L.A.'s most ritzy?" She tilted her head in the direction of the Banquet Center. "We can have a little action of our own."

I shrugged. "Uh huh...I guess."

April grinned and pumped her fist. "You're on."

"Shouldn't you be getting business cards at some point?" I asked, nervous that an April with too much time on her hands might decide to intervene on behalf of the universe.

April bounced to her feet. "You're right!"

April made like she was about to walk away with the cards still in her hands.

"Wait, we can still finish our game."

"Oh, right," April looked around like she just remembered where she was. "Um..."

I waved my hand dismissively. "Actually, don't worry about it. I'll be okay."

"Are you sure?"

"Yeah, crappy luck tonight anyway." I placed my cards onto the remaining deck. "I'll get myself some air. I won't be long."

Mr. Thorne

Finding a private space to get some air turned out to be more challenging than I expected. After getting lost and circling the same floor twice, I finally came to the conclusion that I should ask the front desk downstairs. Fortunately, once reception gave me the directions, it didn't take me too long to find a cozy tea garden, tucked out of the way in the south hall.

Stepping up to the swinging glass doors, I could already feel my shoulders relaxing. It was time to decompress and put tonight into the jar of embarrassing moments that I would never again revisit.

As I put my hand on the handle, I heard a distinct masculine voice behind me say, "It's you."

It didn't take too much imagination to figure out whose voice it was. I instinctively froze, trying to run through my options, but they were severely limited after I made eye contact with the reflection in the glass door.

"Nev, right?" Ethan Thorne asked.

There was only one person who called me Nev. How the hell did he know that was April's nickname for me? Had she sold me out? It hadn't been that long since I last saw her. Could she have made a beeline from the stairwell right to Ethan? And how the hell had he found me here?

Think about it Sierra, how many quiet balconies can there possibly be in this hotel? if April spilled the beans on where you were headed, it would've been a doozy to track you down.

I got a hold of myself and turned as calmly as possible. I'd deal with April later, right now I had another problem on my hands.

Ethan held my gaze when I came to face him. There was a curious smirk on his face.

Act surprised Sierra, you don't remember who he is, you don't want it to seem like you remember him from somewhere other than earlier today. He's calling you Nev, so he probably doesn't know who you are. Be professional!

"Oh, Mr. Thorne!" My voice had caught a little too high-pitched, but I went with it. "If there is something you need, you can speak with the event coordinator. Her name is Giselle, I would be more than happy to fetch her for you."

Without waiting for a reply I took a step toward the nearest escalator, but Ethan stopped me, his hand pressed lightly against the inside of my elbow.

I nearly jumped into the air, but his touch made me spin into him, until we were in each other's personal space. His face was close enough that I could smell something that reminded me of high backed leather armchairs and bourbon. Heat rushed to my cheeks and I hesitated for a moment too long.

"No, you misunderstand," Ethan said, his deep voice rumbling through my body.

My eyes inadvertently dropped to his pants. They were the exact same shade of blue that I'd remembered earlier in the Banquet Center, but the wet splash was gone. Of course, the blonde woman must've taken him to change. He probably had an extra pair of pants specifically for occasions where klutzy flower girls fell all over his chest. With a jolt, I realized that I was staring at his crotch and quickly darted my eyes back to his face.

Ethan watched me without acknowledging my interest in his groin region. A strange look passed across his face. Had that been a flash of recognition or did I imagine it? The only thing worse than spilling stinky flower water on the most recognizable guest at a charity event was having him remember all the embarrassing stuff you two did as kids.

Pull it together Sierra! Of course he doesn't recognize you, he's just upset about having his pants ruined.

Donning my professional smile, I nodded politely then took a careful step back to put some distance between us.

"Please accept my deepest apologies for the accident earlier," I said.

A smile crinkled the corner of Ethan's eyes. I was on the right track. He'd been unhappy with the treatment he received, wanted to set things straight, and was finally satisfied with my change in attitude.

"I'm glad to see you've found a fresh pair of pants," I said, "I will be more than happy to cover the dry cleaning costs for the other pair."

"No, that won't be necessary," he said, with a dismissive wave of his hand.

"Then if there's anything else you need assistance with—"

"How about a drink?"

"A d-drink?" I asked, unable to keep the confusion from my face.

Ethan shrugged. "Order me a drink and we'll call it even."

"You...want me to get you a drink," I said flatly.

Ethan nodded.

I took a deep breath. My paranoia had gotten the best of me earlier. He hadn't been looking for me at all, he'd probably come to the tea garden with the same idea I had, seeking a private corner to relax, and had run into me by accident. Now he just wanted someone to bring him a drink so he could enjoy his peace and quiet.

As for how he knew to call me "Nev," he'd probably overheard April at some point.

"Okay, what would you like?" I asked. If all he wanted was for me to fetch him a drink, that was easy enough.

"Your choice."

"Fine, I'll be right back," I said.

I walked past him toward the Banquet Center.

Ethan's footsteps echoed behind me.

I stopped and turned around, confused again.

"Um..."

"I'm coming with you," he offered as way of explanation.

If he was walking with me all the way to the bar, then what was the point of having me get him the drink?

"You do know that, as a guest, you can order a drink for yourself right?" I offered politely, "There's an open bar right by the table games," I added, in case he had missed it.

"Good," he said simply.

I didn't want to offend him, but I wasn't sure if perhaps he had so much money that he didn't know how open bars worked. A guy like that probably never carried any cash around. Instead of paying for anything directly, he had people who handled all of that for him.

I didn't want to assume, but sometimes with the ultra-wealthy, you never knew.

"Um, complimentary," I further clarified, "Free. As in, you can tell the bartender what you want and they'll serve it to you."

Ethan nodded. "Yes, that would be ordering a drink for myself. I want you to order a drink for me."

This guy.

I turned away for a moment to compose myself. Ethan didn't just want to kick back in the tea garden and have me fetch him a drink. He was doing this to be purposefully difficult.

This was some kind of power trip to get back at me for earlier.

It made me feel stupid for telling April that Ethan was only a sweet nerdy boy who happened to grow up and become a Fortune 500 CEO. Now I realized that he was just as much of a prick as every other entitled trust fund baby. Actually, Ethan had always had a weird streak when we were kids, coming up with the most absurd games, so I suppose he hadn't grown out of that.

But I would have much preferred that version of Ethan over this one.

The more I learned about "Mr. Thorne," the less I wanted to find out.

He gestured toward the hallway leading back to the Banquet Center. "Shall we?"

I drew in a slow, steady breath.

As much as it irritated me, if he wanted me to order him a drink from the open bar for dirtying his pants, then I was getting off the hook relatively easy.

I strode down the hall without checking if Ethan was following me, but I could feel his silent presence behind me all the same.

We approached the side of the casino floor and I located the bar. Unlike the open bars at events that April and I were used to attending, the crowd tonight was much classier, so there wasn't a line stretched halfway around the block waiting to get free booze.

In fact, there was hardly anyone around and the bartender looked a little bored, waiting patiently with both hands behind his back. He was a somber, older man with high cheekbones, wearing an old school saloon vest. I recognized him from our mad dash to move the equipment from the Royal Ballroom to the Banquet Center, he'd been pulling a dolly piled high with coolers out of the service elevator.

The bartender's eyes lit up the moment he spotted us and he started moving to meet our approach.

Before I could even speak, the bartender pulled out a leather box, opened it, and presented the velvet-cushioned bottle inside. Ignoring me completely, he said to Ethan, "Mr. Thorne, may I offer a pour of the Glenn Mackay, fifty-five year, compliments of the Conservation Fund?"

Recognizing my exit, I jumped on the opportunity to bow out gracefully.

"It looks like you will be well taken care of Mr. Thorne. Enjoy your evening."

"Please call me Ethan," he said, "and you haven't made good on your word, Nev."

For a moment, his eyes darkened as if he saw into my soul and every moment of our past was illuminated. A chill raced up my spine. Of course he meant when I agreed to order him a drink just now. He wasn't talking about the past. He would have definitely said something if he recognized me, I told myself.

I spun around, fists clenched. "You're actually serious."

Ethan raised a hand to the bartender, "Hold the Glenn Mackay, but pass my gratitude to the host. Nev will order for me."

Then he took a seat on the bar stool, looking at me expectantly. The bartender played along, but flashed me a confused look.

I stood there for a moment fuming. Ethan's stubborn insistence on seeing this thing through was bringing back familiar emotions. Maybe he hadn't changed much at all. Then again, I didn't remember ever getting *this* pissed off at him. I wondered if it had anything to do with the fact that now he was an irritatingly attractive billionaire that put the tuxedo he was wearing to shame?

Regardless, I wasn't about to let any version of Ethan Thorne, past or present, get one over on me.

"Mr. Thorne will have a Cosmopolitan," I said to the bartender, smiling with all my teeth.

Cosmos had been April's favorite drink since college. I usually stuck to Diet Coke, preferring to save my allocation of carbs to something I would actually enjoy, like bread sticks.

Let the big bad Ethan Thorne be seen enjoying *that*.

Ethan shrugged. "I'm in her hands." Then motioning smoothly to the bartender, he said, "And if you could pour the Glenn Mackay for Nev, please."

What the hell kind of game was he trying to play here?

I placed a firm hand on the bar to make sure the bartender wouldn't miss anything. "Don't bother," I said, "I'm needed in the back."

"Please," Ethan said, putting a hand on my arm before I could leave. "I believe I owe you my thanks."

I opened my mouth to say something cutting, but instead stood there confused. Thank me? For what? Ordering him a fruity cocktail that was popular at bachelorette parties?

"Uh...sorry?" I managed.

Ethan leaned casually against the bar. "I've been involved with the Conservation Fund for many years," he said, "I appreciate what you've done tonight."

He looked at me with an earnest smile. At that moment he almost looked like the young Ethan I'd once known and an overwhelming wave of nostalgia washed over me. I wasn't sure how to respond.

"Well, I'm glad you enjoy the flowers," I said eventually.

Ethan scoffed. "Don't sell yourself short," he opened his arms and turned to the murmuring casino tables behind him, "the guests are having a grand time. They've completely forgotten tonight's event was initially located in the Royal Ballroom. Creating such an experience is challenging in the best of times, never mind contending with a last minute disaster. As I understand it, you voluntarily stepped into the chaos to help make this possible. So if there is anyone who deserves the Glenn Mackay, it's you."

I stuttered, feeling my cheeks flush, and tried to search for an appropriate response.

It was hard not to be flattered by those words. I scanned his face for a sign that he was just trying to butter me up, but his expression matched his tone. He really did mean what he said. Had I judged him too harshly before? But more importantly, how the hell did he know so much about my role in helping Giselle save the event?

Ethan smiled at someone over my shoulder. I turned to see who it was, taking advantage of the distraction.

April was scampering over, the bottom of her dress fluttering about, flashing her eyes at me as if she needed to unload some deep dark secret.

Either that, or to confess a mortal sin.

Why was I not surprised? The puzzle pieces were starting to come together.

"Nev!" she squeaked excitedly when she joined us at the bar and then caught herself. "Nev," she said more calmly this time. "I just wanted to let you know that I have everything under control and you can leave the breakdown to me. I also spoke to Giselle, who agrees that you deserve to take it easy for the rest of the event," she enunciated clearly, speaking loudly enough for Ethan to catch every word.

There was no telling what else she might do in Ethan's presence so I pulled April to the opposite corner of the bar. Had she acted as the hand of the universe to bring Ethan and me together? If so, we were about to have some words.

"What the hell is going on?" I whisper-shouted when we were far enough away. "You went out of your way to blab about me?"

"No-no," she protested, "as soon as I got back to the vendor lounge, I saw him wandering around asking for you! So—"

"So you went up to him and told him my entire life story?"

April shook her head, "No, I knew that if he found Giselle, she would've told him your *real name*. First and last. She doesn't know to hide your identity from him, so I had to give him *something* to make him leave."

"And that's when you told him my nickname."

"I had to get him out of there before Giselle showed up!"

I wanted to say something angry but nothing came out. In the end, I grumbled, "Great, now he's under the impression that I saved the day, even though Giselle's in charge."

"Well, you kind of did, didn't you?"

"I helped, but—"

"Aw Nev, don't be mad," she whined. "You know I babble when I'm nervous." She held her right hand up like she was on the witness stand. "But I swear, that's all I told him."

I couldn't really blame her, especially under these circumstances. I looked back over my shoulder. Ethan was chatting easily to the bartender, but he still glanced over to us from time to time. He smiled when he saw me looking his way.

I sighed and turned back to April. "Okay, okay," I said, surrendering. "You did the best you could, considering."

She immediately broke into a wide grin. "So I still have a seat in your time machine?"

"I get to decide what time period we go to though, I don't want to end up in one of your Regencies."

April positioned herself so that she would be out of view from Ethan on the other end of the bar. Her eyes glinted mischievously. "I told you he'd recognize you."

"I seriously doubt that."

"Even without your name he recognizes something familiar about you, like a—" April's eyelashes fluttered, "like an indescribable feeling deep in his being."

"Deep in his being, huh?"

April leaned over my shoulder to get a good glimpse of Ethan, then gave me a coy look. "Remember our bet?"

"In the stairwell?"

April nodded. "Wouldn't you say I've won?"

"You're kidding right? He's only interested in me because he thinks I saved the day, plus I spilled water on his crotch. It is definitely *not* because he recognizes me."

"He just needs a bit more time," she shrugged. Then she started flipping her hand back and forth on the bartop making sizzling noises. "I can almost smell the L.A. Kalbi already," she taunted.

I was getting sick and tired of April not dropping the Ethan issue. It was past time to set her straight.

"Don't count your Kalbi before it hits the grill," I said. "Alright, I'll show you that Ethan doesn't have *any* idea who I am. I'm going to have this one drink with him, and he's not going to notice a thing. And after, I don't want to hear another word from you about *Mr. Thorne* ever again. Got it?"

"Sure, a deal's a deal." April handed me the long blazer I kept in the van. I hadn't noticed until that moment that she had been holding it, and now she was giving it to me like she'd known I'd give in.

She held her palm out to collect my work apron, which I grudgingly handed to her.

"Have fun," she said. She poked me in the ribs playfully, then scampered away.

Tit for Tat

After April left, I took a moment to compose myself. All I had to do was make it through one drink with Ethan to win the bet and then I'd be dining on juicy, marinated Korean BBQ this weekend. Besides, April, Giselle, and even Ethan thought that I deserved to take it easy for helping out. Who was I to argue with that?

I returned to Ethan's side of the bar. The drinks had not been prepared yet, as if Ethan had frozen the moment in time.

"Shall we continue where we left off?" he asked. His tone indicated that he never had a single doubt that I'd return. Where had Ethan learned such self-assurance? There was just something so infuriating about his demeanor that made me want to see *him* off balance for a change.

"Sure," I said. I turned my attention to the bartender, "Mr. Thorne will enjoy his Cosmopolitan now."

Just because I was here to prove April wrong, didn't mean that I had to put up with all of Ethan's bullshit. I hadn't forgotten his little power trip of making me order him a drink, and I wasn't about to let him off the hook.

Without missing a beat, Ethan nodded and the bartender went to work. I noted with annoyance that the bartender had waited for *Ethan's* go ahead instead of mine.

It only took a minute for the bartender to prepare the Cosmopolitan and pour the Glenn Mackay. He set them down on the counter in front of us before drifting away to attend to the other guests, leaving the two of us alone.

The Cosmopolitan was perfect. The pretty pink cocktail came in a slim wedge shaped glass with a slice of lime balanced on the rim.

Ethan considered what I'd ordered him, as if deciding his angle of attack.

Let's see him try to drink *that* like he was James Bond. I watched him carefully to see if I could find a chink in his armor of suave nonchalance.

Ethan swept his drink off the bar, his fingers wrapping powerfully around the thin glass stem. He flashed me an easygoing smile, and held the Cosmo up in a toast. "To the tamer of chaos."

He means me. I'm the tamer of chaos.

I hadn't thought about it that way, but if I had already tamed an impossible situation, then how hard could it be to tame Ethan Thorne for the duration of one drink?

Growing bolder, I motioned to the nearby banner of a tiger with the Conservation Fund logo on it and said, "To big cats."

I grabbed my drink — the Glenn Mackay something-something year — like how I imagined a sophisticated man might, clinked my glass against Ethan's, and took a gulp. My mouth instantly felt numb from the spiciness. I forced the liquid down without tasting it, which did little for the burning.

Grimacing, I pounded the glass back down onto the bartop and then turned away to cough into the back of my hand. Jeez, when was the last time I had hard liquor?

Ethan didn't seem to notice or pretended not to notice. He took a pensive sip of the Cosmo, moved his lips slowly, like he was chewing, then swallowed and set his drink down.

"Quite," he paused for a moment, involuntarily pinching his lips together, "tart."

I studied him to see if he possessed any hint of self-consciousness, but he didn't even seem to notice the rest of the room.

Then again, if he cracked that easily, I would've been disappointed.

Still, I was pretty sure I caught an eye twitch there. Was there more of the boy I had known in Mr. Thorne than I'd previously thought? How much had Ethan changed, and how much had remained the same? Might one drink be enough to find out who the *real* Ethan Thorne was?

His hand still on the Cosmo glass, he pointed his index finger at my scotch. "How do you find the Glenn Mackay?"

The only whiskey I was familiar with was the kind that came mixed in a Coke, so to me, the fancy scotch tasted much like paint thinner. The drink was too high-shelf for my unsophisticated palate. I might've felt guilty about not being able to appreciate the drink, but then again, I hadn't asked for any of this. Ethan had insisted.

Which gave me an idea.

I reached over the bar, to where the bartender kept his materials and snatched a couple of ice cubes from the tray. If Ethan was a connoisseur of fine Scotches then I'm sure he had an entire set of preferences for their enjoyment.

He had always been particular, so I wouldn't have expected anything less from him. When we were young, he was always lecturing me about shoulds and shouldn'ts, rules and consequences.

If my hunch was right, then this would drive him up the wall.

"Not bad," I said with a shrug. "A bit too strong though, probably better if I diluted it." I dangled a single ice cube over my whiskey.

"The Glenn Mackay Fifty-Five year is hard to come by these days, most people —"

I dropped the ice into the whiskey without glancing his way. It made a satisfying plop in the amber liquid.

" — prefer to enjoy it straight."

Making a show of it, I swirled the glass around to accelerate the melting, then took a sip. I hadn't given the ice enough time, but that was hardly the point.

"Straight, huh?" I plopped the second cube in, and took another sip. Over the rim of the glass, I looked innocently at Ethan, trying my best to channel April's puppy eyes.

He stared back at me, silent. There was a darkness in his half-lidded gaze. His mouth worked, probably deciding how to tell me off, but he continued to regard me, quiet and still.

For a brief moment, panic thudded in my chest. Had I crossed a line? Gone too far? Images of Ethan telling all his buddies at the country club to blacklist our shop flashed through my mind, but his expression suddenly shifted.

His eyes moved to the whiskey glass, then back to me, crinkling in amusement.

"So," he said, "what do you taste?"

What do I taste? Maybe I had overestimated how well I knew Ethan. After all, it had only been a short summer.

Thinking quickly, I slid the glass over to him, stalling for time. "Help yourself."

He lifted the scotch up to his nose and inhaled deeply. He tilted the glass up for a reserved sip and I noticed my lipstick stain on the opposite side of the rim. Daringly close to his mouth.

He held the glass still for a moment.

Then he closed his eyes and took a deeper draft. Savored it.

After what seemed like an eternity his eyes opened again. His pupils refocused slowly, as if he were returning from a dream or a memory. His face was brimming with something warmer than the intensity of before. It was something new. An expression that I had never seen in all the photographs that April had shown me.

"I've never quite experienced the Glenn Mackay in that way before," he said, finally setting the whiskey down, "How interesting."

He smiled at me.

I'd put the ice in there as a way to needle him, but now he was taking this far more seriously than I'd expected.

Not certain of what it was, but sensing that there was some imperceptible shift in the conversation, I decided to make my exit.

"Please, have the rest of it, then. It would have been wasted on me anyway."

I slipped off the barstool.

"Wait," Ethan said, reaching into his pocket. He leaned closer into the space between us. In one smooth move, he took something out of his pocket and set it on the bar.

Sweeten the Pot

On the bartop sat a tall stack of multicolored casino chips.

"What's this?" I asked, eyebrow raised. Even though I'd been planning on leaving, I didn't.

Ethan nodded toward the table games. "Let's gamble."

"I don't think having me around is going to improve your chances," I said, eyeing the stack coolly, trying to not make it seem like I was lingering, that I could be talked into staying. A number of the chips were oversized, probably indicating pricier bets. Though the younger Ethan had always been competitive, I had a feeling that the Ethan the CEO *really* played to win. The last thing I wanted was to be responsible for losing his money after already ruining his pants. I gave him a genuinely concerned look. "It'd be a poor investment."

"And why is that?"

"Don't tell me you forgot what happened earlier. What if my bad luck rubs off on you?"

Ethan slid the stack—and the half finished glass of whiskey—across the polished wood countertop until they rested next to my elbow. "The best business decisions always seem bad if you look at them from the wrong angle."

"Spoken like a man who's made some bad decisions," I shot back.

Ethan chuckled and shook his head, playing it off. I gave myself a mental pat on the back. If I'd learned anything tonight, it was that he was still human after all.

"The evening's proceeds go to the Conservation Fund. We're not in Vegas; the table games are just a way for us to amuse ourselves." He lifted his Cosmo glass, took a fruity sip, and peered over the rim at me. "So how about it?"

It was hard to see Ethan as the dangerous playboy April seemed to think he was when he held his Cosmo like that. Still, I had to remind myself, Cosmos were not his drink of choice. He was accustomed to having Glenn Mackay, straight.

I looked down at the whiskey and the casino chips.

How much did each one of those chips represent? A hundred dollars? No way, too low stakes for this event. A thousand dollars? We were getting closer. Maybe ten thousand? I didn't even want to think about it. The numbers were starting to make me nauseous.

Expensive whiskey and high stakes gambling. When I looked at it that way, I *could* see the dangerous playboy in the tabloids and April's imagination.

Did I really want to get sucked into that world? Besides, how much did I truly know about him anyway? It was clear that neither of us were children any more. Whether we'd changed for the better or the worse was still up for debate. I couldn't deny that I was tempted by the prospect of spending more time with Ethan to answer that question for the sake of my curiosity, but in the end, reason won out.

I remembered the blonde in the form fitting charcoal dress that had escorted Ethan away in the lobby area. If he had come here with a date, what kind of person would I be to step into that mess?

I shoved the stack of chips—which had ballooned to the value of twenty million dollars in my imagination—back across the bartop, next to his Cosmo.

"Don't you have your date to attend to?" I asked.

"My date?" He looked confused.

"The lady you were with."

His eyes relaxed in recognition. "Ah, you mean my assistant."

An assistant? I thought about it for a moment. That did make sense, she was wearing a rather muted dress and walked around as if she held some invisible clipboard to her chest.

Ethan plucked the top chip off the stack and fingered it playfully before placing it back. "Dates don't usually keep you on schedule and screen your phone calls, you know."

"Some might, if you're into that," I said, cheekily.

Ethan tapped the plastic chips and flashed me a sly look. "Are *you* into that?"

"What, having someone tell me what to do?" I shrugged and took a sip of my drink. "If I wanted a man to bark orders at me, I wouldn't be working for myself."

Ethan nodded. "Of course, you're a business woman." He slid the chips to the center of the space in between us. "Let's talk business then. What'll it take to convince you to spend some time at the tables with me?"

Our back and forth was getting a little too intense for me. The smart thing would've been to step away. Instead, I turned to watch the crowd of glitzy philanthropists milling around the casino tables.

Out there, in the middle of all those extravagantly dressed people, I'd stick out like a sore thumb in my blazer and slacks. Not only that, but half of them must've seen me humiliate myself earlier. It was all risk and no reward.

Still, maybe there *was* a way I could turn this to my advantage.

It was my turn to play idly with the top chip of the stack as I eyed Ethan's Cosmopolitan. He'd almost finished it, there was only a small layer of pink liquid left at the bottom of the glass.

"Maybe there is something you can offer me," I teased, not wanting to overplay it now that I had a plan.

Ethan leaned back and spread his arms open graciously. "I'm all ears."

I'd been enjoying my conversation with Ethan and not even once did a glimmer of recognition cross his eyes. After he'd had a good look at me, surely he would have said something by now if he "recognized something deep in his soul." I could almost picture April stuffing Korean BBQ into her mouth, sulkily.

As far as I was concerned, I'd already won the bet.

But what would be a more brilliant topping to that sweet victory than parading Ethan around the casino floor while he sipped on April's favorite drink?

"I pick the bets," I started, "and —"

"Deal," he said before I could finish.

"Hold on, there's more. For every one of these chips I win," I picked up a small black one, "you order another Cosmopolitan. For yourself this time. My debt for ruining your pants has already been paid."

Ethan smirked, his eyes inscrutable. He stroked the slender stem of the glass, considering it. "Are you trying to get me drunk?"

I lifted the scotch and pretended to smell it pretentiously like I'd seen him do earlier. "We're just amusing ourselves," I said, before taking a sip. "So how about it?"

Ethan tossed back the rest of the Cosmo in one gulp. "And if you lose? You did say that you have bad luck."

I shrugged playfully. "Just one more bad decision to add to your portfolio, I suppose."

"Depends on how you look at it," he said, grinning.

I allowed myself a small smile. My heart pounded. He had actually taken the bait. The great Ethan Thorne, on the hook.

My hook.

Before I could lose my nerve, I palmed the chips in my left hand, took the scotch in my right, and headed for the nearest table.

Not once did it cross my mind that perhaps it wasn't Ethan who was on the hook that night.

Kiss Goodbye

Five Cosmopolitans later and *after* I made certain that April had finally gotten a good look at us, Ethan and I decided that we'd both had enough gambling for the evening. I must have used up all of my bad luck on the accident earlier and all that remained was good fortune. My winning streak surprised even myself. Maybe the universe was finally conspiring for my benefit for once.

Ethan swung us by the reception area up front where he donated all of his winnings to the Conservation Fund. The evening was starting to wind down and April had texted me, insisting that she wanted to handle tear down by herself, ending with a "call me if you need me" and a bunch of winky faces.

Ethan and I wandered close to the main entrance of the Banquet Center where he could have a seat on the too-avante-garde-for-comfort sofas. I went to the bar, ordered two glasses of ice water and brought them back.

We sipped them in companionable silence, basking in the afterglow of our fun, when Ethan's attention was suddenly perked.

"Quick, help me up," he said.

"What's wrong?" I asked as I grabbed his arm to help him balance.

"Past the bar," he nodded toward my right.

I glanced over to see his assistant striding across the room. Though she was dressed simply, she moved with noticeable elegance and grace. So much so that she was getting a lot of appraising looks from the men. She seemed not to notice the attention directed her way, instead swiveling her head back and forth like she was on a mission.

"Seems like your date must need you for something."

"I know that look," Ethan said, grimacing at my joke, "If she finds me, I'll be dragged into an insufferable conversation with some financier." He grabbed my hand. "Come on, we need to get out of here."

I shrugged and went along with it. "The big bad CEO hiding from his assistant," I teased as I let him lead us into the lobby area just outside the Banquet Center.

"Discretion is the better part of valor and all that," Ethan said. He closed the door behind him with dramatic care.

Now that Ethan was safe from his assistant, I took some time to study our surroundings. I remembered power-walking through the area during the early stages of set up when it had still been bare and random equipment was piled up all over the place. Now, the lobby looked completely transformed.

The Conservation Fund had gone through no small trouble to set up an elaborate display. A velvet red carpet rope protected a taxidermied panther in full hunting motion, clawing at a rabbit. Plants had been arranged on the platform to resemble a grassland. The panther was frozen mid snarl, the points of its canines exposed.

I walked over to the placard next to the display.

"Zola," Ethan said, nodding at the panther.

"Sorry?"

Ethan joined me by the placard, thumbing the plastic as if he were reading it. "Her name was Zola. She was abandoned by her mother and found by land surveyors. By the time they rescued her, she was too old to develop the proper instincts to be released into the wild. Most of her life was spent at the San Diego zoo. It was the best conservationists could do for her at that point."

Ethan looked almost wistful as he spoke about this animal, as if she were a beloved family pet. It was fascinating to see this side of him. For some reason I doubted that he was reading from the information printed on the colorful display.

"You're speaking like you knew her."

Ethan shrugged. "I saw her. Once. As a child."

"Must've left quite an impression," I offered, slightly uncomfortable with Ethan reminiscing too much about the past.

"Even caged, she was magnificent." Ethan's eyes focused into the distance, turning glassy.

We stood there in silence, the two of us standing awkwardly in front of the taxidermied animals. I wanted to say something that would cheer him up.

"You think she'll ever catch the stuffed rabbit?" I joked, pointing to the animal.

Ethan chuckled, returning from whatever memory he had been lost in.

He turned to me as if remembering something suddenly and looked at me with soft eyes. When he spoke, his voice was low, achingly intimate. "I enjoyed our time tonight. When can I see you again?"

I broke our gaze and took a step toward the display. This moment of nature captured in time was far safer than the dangerous words slipping out of Ethan's mouth. My heart urged me to run, to flee like the rabbit. But my feet remained planted in place.

In this moment, we were still strangers. Somehow it felt safer that way. If we saw each other again, things would change. And at some point he would remember it all. Would he feel the same way about me then?

Ethan stepped next to me, close enough for me to feel his body heat radiating against my upper arm. He remained silent, but he was tense, waiting for an answer.

My skin yearned to touch his. I tilted my head up slightly to see his face, making the decision before doubt could slip in. His lips looked plush and soft, a hint of stubble framing his chin.

"Why don't we just enjoy the moment?" I said.

I tiptoed up to meet him. His lips were heaven against mine and my mouth lingered a moment longer than it had any right to. He smelled of oak and grass and wildflowers, like deep dark wood and mid-morning sun, like a place that only existed in fantasy.

And then it was over.

I retreated before he could pull me deeper. My chest felt empty. A void that spanned the many years we'd been apart. Tonight had been surreal, but now it was time to say goodbye.

Ethan's eyes met mine insistently. "I'll need more than a moment."

This time it was Ethan who leaned in. He held my face between his hands. The motion caught me off guard, but when we crashed together, everything was forgotten. The room. The accident. The games. This kiss was more desperate, more urgent than before, like he would devour me if I let him. Maybe I wanted him to.

Against my cheeks, his hands felt rough and calloused. I wondered how they got that way. Surely someone in his position didn't need to do any manual labor. Was it from working out? Did he do any martial arts? Woodchopping?

There was so much about him that I still didn't know, that I would never know.

We would remain as strangers forever.

We finally broke free, both of us gasping. A strand of hair fell across Ethan's forehead, slashing across his eyes.

That's when I saw it in his face. That it would never be enough for him. That he wanted all of me.

I couldn't help but see it as a childish desire, a craving, a need that I couldn't fulfill. We were just children then, too shy and unsure of ourselves. Of course there would never have been a kiss, but would that goodbye have felt just like this? I never found out how he felt about it at the time, but now that I could see it, maybe this would be the goodbye that never was.

"Take us somewhere," I whispered into the scruff of his neck, leaving a kiss on his skin.

He tensed, but he didn't pull back.

I ran my hands up the back of his suit, feeling the cords of tight muscle beneath the fabric. "Now."

Ethan studied me hard, still recovering from the kiss. Conflict contorted his face, but nature won out. "Okay," he finally whispered.

He placed his hand on the small of my back, guiding me. We savored each step, knowing where it would inevitably lead. We didn't need to rush and we didn't need to stall.

Neither of us broke the silence as the elevator doors closed. Ethan pressed the floor number and backed into the left corner. I chose the opposite corner. He didn't come any closer. It was as if in that enclosed, private space together, we were afraid of standing too close, for fear of what would happen if we touched.

A couple of shy kids at a middle school dance. Making up for lost time.

The floors rushed past. The elevator slowed. Stopped.

Then the doors opened.

Loose Ends

One night to tie up one summer of loose ends.

Maybe this was the closure that we both needed.

That I needed.

In a way, it would be fitting, I managed to convince myself.

We walked out of the elevator and down the hall, Ethan leading the way. The sounds of our steps were muted into the plush carpet. It was quiet enough for me to hear my heart beating. Or perhaps my heart was beating too loudly. To repress my restless mind, I focused on Ethan's shoulders. They seemed broader, the hallway narrower.

We stopped in front of the suite, the recessed yellow lighting made the door appear intimidating, like a gateway into another world.

Ethan pulled a keycard from the inside pocket of his tuxedo jacket. He played with the plastic between his fingers, hesitating on the threshold. What was he waiting for? Did he think that we were moving too fast?

I took a silent shuddering breath and leaned into him. Through the fabric, I could feel the muscles of his back tensing against my breasts. Anticipation coiled in my belly. Need ached between my thighs.

Ethan stood like a statue, his lips pressed into a firm line.

Perhaps he was taking all of this a little too seriously. He wanted to savor the chase. To enjoy the dance. Ethan Thorne was still trying to play all his cards right when the game was already settled in my mind.

I snatched the keycard from him and stepped in front so he couldn't see my hand tremble.

I made the choice for the both of us.

The lock flashed from red to green, then clicked open.

Ethan grabbed my hand over the doorknob. "Wait," he said.

Before I could change my mind, I pushed into the room and pulled Ethan inside.

The door swung shut behind us.

We made it as far as a couple of steps into the entryway before I pressed my entire body against him. Our lips connected. Needy and urgent.

Ethan returned the kiss, first meeting my challenge, then claiming my mouth with desire. Even though we were focused on the implied communication of our lips, I could feel the bursting tingles of warmth spreading across my body.

My knees felt weak, ready to spill me onto the ground. My nipples hardened. Heat pooled down in my core. I was putty in his hands. At that moment, if he wanted me, he could have had me and I would have offered no resistance.

But instead, Ethan retreated, slamming his back against the opposite wall. My eyes adjusted to the dim lighting diffusing over from the living room in the suite.

"Don't push me." He raked his hand through his dark locks, catching his breath. "You won't like it."

The need between my thighs only ached hotter, making me bold, careless. Even as my pulse roared in my ears, something in me wanted to go just a little too far, push a little too hard. I wanted to unravel his facade. I wanted to reveal the core of Ethan Thorne.

Stepping up to him, I rubbed my hand against his crotch. "I'm not interested in playing games," I said, feeling him through the thin fabric straining at half mast.

Ethan's eyes went wide and his breath caught in his chest.

I smirked at him. "And you don't seem too interested in playing games either."

Shaking my blazer off, I reached down to my midriff and almost tore my blouse off. The vents overhead blew cold air across my naked skin and I would have shivered if it weren't for the heat between us and my hungry impatience.

"You're out of control." His voice rumbled low, his eyes drinking my cleavage, bared and exposed to him.

No, I wasn't out of control *enough*.

"What are you going to do about it?" I unbuttoned his tuxedo, tearing it off of his shoulders.

He grasped my upper arm, his rough hand like a brand against my cool skin.

"You going to hold me down?" I asked, untying his bow tie, pulling him to me by his collar. I bit his bottom lip, almost hard enough to draw blood. "Tie me up?" I teasingly suggested.

He growled. "Is that what you want?" His eyes glimmered dangerously in the light.

A dark promise.

I let the fear move through me for a moment, then pushed it down. We were past the point of no return, for me, if not for him.

"Is that what *you* want?" I threw back at him.

Before I knew it, I was reaching for his pants. Ethan moved his hands to my wrists, gripping them tightly enough to hurt.

We weren't playing anymore.

I wrenched my shoulders away, pulling and twisting against his strength. My elbow connected with his sternum and we both went down. Our limbs tangled together on the floor, but I came out on top.

I sat up, straddling his legs. Frantically, I scrabbled for his belt, my fingers working. His abs tightened, like he was getting ready to get up. I pushed his chest back down with both hands.

He didn't like that.

Ethan rolled his body over on top of me, the fine fabric of his dress shirt pressed against my bare skin. His eyes glinted in the low light, intense, questioning. If he hadn't been on top of me, those eyes alone would have trapped me. His knee lifted between my legs and I spread myself for him, letting him touch me there. I whimpered, grinding against him, heat flooding my cheeks.

In a flash, his hands were on me, his fingers digging into my sides. He flipped me over like I weighed nothing, until I was face down on the floor. Ethan on top of me, his body holding me down, pressing my breasts against the scratchy rug. Then I felt his erection, unyielding and hot against my back. My heart pounded, a surge of heat pooling in my belly. We both paused for a moment to catch our breaths, the air cooling a slick sheen of sweat on my skin.

His weight shifted above me, and then there was only pressure on the small of my back. I squirmed, trying to escape, but I was pinned against the floor, completely helpless. I craned my neck back, trying to see what he was doing, but could only see the side of the ornately carved wooden couch.

Ethan hiked my pants up, by my right ankle. There was something tender and erotic about his motions, even though I couldn't see anything. I closed my eyes savoring the sensations. Something slippery and cool snaked around my ankle, once, twice, then knotted firmly against my skin.

Panic rose in my chest.

I thought we were just horsing around but he was really tying me up.

Where had he even gotten the rope?

But wasn't this what I wanted? What I'd been pushing for?

"Wait," I protested, fear overcoming the arousal.

Abruptly, all of his weight was gone, and despite my fear, I felt myself mourning an absence.

I flipped over, scrambling to my feet. I propped myself against the arm of the couch and crossed my arms defensively in front of my breasts, trying to retain whatever dignity I had left. Even though I'd initiated the game of chicken, now *I* was the one who got too scared.

Ethan stood a safe distance away, chest heaving, hair tousled. His face was clouded with emotion. He lifted his eyes slowly, raking them over my body, before resting them at my gaze.

I broke away, looking down. There, on my ankle was a crimson ribbon tied into a neat bow. With a start, the realization came flooding back. It was the same ribbon that he had pocketed earlier in the evening. He held onto *that* the entire evening? But why would he…

Ethan was staring at me intently, his eyes shiny in the darkness, his chest breathing hard, his cock clearly straining against the thin fabric of his pants.

He said, "I've let you have your fun, Sierra."

Sierra.
Sierra.

My own name echoed in my head. Blood pounded in my ears, making me feel dizzy. I blinked, trying to fight the growing numbness in my chest, acting as if it meant nothing. As if he hadn't just said my name. As if he didn't know who I was the entire evening. I bent down, fumbling with the silk ribbon, trying to untie it, to undo the past.

"Don't," he commanded, almost grunted. "This time, you're the one who will have to wait."

The hairs on the back of my neck tingled.

I froze, unsure. Waiting. Watching, as Ethan Thorne took one shuddering breath, walked to the door and left the room.

Mr. Thorne will return...

...but if you can't *wait*

...then sign up for my mailing list at
http://lkrayne.com
to receive **Thorne One**,
an EXCLUSIVE BONUS SCENE from Mr.
Thorne's perspective.

This bonus scene will NOT be available
anywhere else...

Dear Lovely Reader,

Thank you so much for reading Silk & Thorne! I've certainly had a blast writing this story and I'm overjoyed that it is finally in your hands.

Stories are my favorite way to connect with people, but sometimes writing a book can feel like a lonely road with sparse feedback along the way.

After the publication of Silk & Thorne, I've been delighted to find that one of the greatest joys of this process has been seeing reviews from readers like yourself. If you loved this story, I'd love to hear about it! What was your favorite scene? Maybe a favorite moment?

Again, thank you so much for taking the time to read my book. There are an endless number of books to choose from, so as an author just starting out, I truly appreciate you giving me a chance! :)

Cheers,
Liv

Mr. Thorne appears in the Silk & Thorne Trilogy:

Silk & Thorne

Satin & Thorne

Lace & Thorne

Satin & Thorne (Silk & Thorne 2)

All it took to upend my entire world, was a single silk ribbon.

The first night I met Ethan Thorne, we'd been hiding behind masks, dancing around the inevitable. I should have been content to watch from afar, to forbid myself from veering too close. But falling into our old patterns felt natural, the promise of a challenge hypnotising me into reckless action.

I'd wanted to say goodbye, to apologize for the pain I'd caused all those years ago, but Ethan wouldn't let me go so easily. With a single silk ribbon, he bound our destinies together.

Now, we begin a new game, around pain and pleasure, with consequences beyond seduction and submission. Will this new game allow us to rediscover our connection and overcome the past or are we condemned to keep repeating the same mistakes?

With our hearts on the line, all we can do is put our masks on, and pretend this game won't change us, won't hurt us, won't end.

Keep reading for an exclusive excerpt from Satin & Thorne (Silk & Thorne 2)…

Ethan wore a casual pair of khaki slacks, a brown belt, and a light blue shirt. Even though he was no longer outfitted in the same formal wear as that night at the charity ball, he was still a sight to behold. His hair was loosely tousled, not messy, yet not formally styled, contrasting with his clean shaven jaw line.

He stopped at the door. I caught a whiff of his cologne with a passing breeze. The scent instantly transported me to that hazy night more than a week ago in the Imperial Grand Hotel when—for a brief moment—we'd been skin against skin, breath against breath, lips against lips.

But now the haze had lifted and everything was illuminated in the light of day.

And on the sunny 5600 block of El Camino in Los Angeles we watched each other awkwardly, him outside my shop, me safely inside, the door ajar between us.

For a beat neither of us knew what to say, but he flashed me a relaxed smile. I suddenly remembered the feeling of his calloused hands, heavy against my ribcage.

Blood rushed to my cheeks and I fought the instinct to pretend like I hadn't seen him.

Fat chance of selling that one.

"Hi," said Ethan.

"I'm sorry, um. We're closed. I mean," I shook my head, "I'm still going to be here, but we're by appointment only after five so... I guess we're not *technically* closed but uh... are you... what are you here for?"

Smooth Sierra, real smooth.

Ethan leaned over in order to avoid talking to me from behind the door and presented his cellphone. There was an email open. I could feel him watching me as I scanned the screen.

The email was a standard confirmation for appointments. Specifically, an appointment at our shop: Venus Floral Design.

My consultation for the evening was *Ethan Thorne*?

But that was ridiculous, I'd checked the appointment book and the name was definitely Stephen Reinsmar. I always made a point of learning my client names before their meetings.

"There must be some sort of mistake," I said scanning the email again. Sure enough, the reservation was for Stephen Reinsmar. "Yes, this confirmation is for someone else."

Ethan cracked a grin at me through the door. "Alter-egos have their uses, especially for someone in my position." He helpfully added, "I'm sure you understand."

Was that a jab at me?

Calling April's nickname for me an "alter-ego" would have been stretching it, but I could see where he might get that idea from.

I reminded myself not to jump to conclusions in my panicked state.

It wasn't that uncommon for celebrities to use pseudonyms to make reservations in order to avoid the paparazzi or crazed fans. Even our little shop had gotten a few of those. Booking an appointment under a different name could have been entirely innocent — Ethan Thorne's standard operating procedure. Either way I had to wrestle with the fact the he'd decided to show up right here at my shop. Of course, I'd expected to hear from Ethan again after how our last meeting had ended, but I still wasn't ready. I thought I'd have more time.

And wasn't Ethan the type of guy who was very busy?

Which begged the question: Why was he here? To talk? Talk about what?

"May I come in?" Ethan asked. "It's a little hot out here."

I realized that I was leaning my entire weight against the barely open door, as if bracing myself against it might be a good defense against having Ethan in my flower shop. At the same moment, I realized that *he* must've been pushing equally hard to keep the door open. Embarrassed, I relented. Ethan, consciously or unconsciously, eased off as well.

"Yes, of course, come in," I said, stepping back and swinging the door open, my mind racing through the possible reasons that Ethan could have wanted to make an appointment. I'd promised April that I'd keep an open mind, and I had resolved to go with the flow, but I wasn't exactly prepared for whatever this was.

And what if he was here to confront me about the past?

Sorry about that minor incident fifteen years ago when I told you we'd run away together but I ditched you instead... Kids do the darndest thing, am I right? P.S. You're a great kisser.

Or what if he was here to talk about the more recent past, when we'd almost had sex in his hotel room?

I couldn't decide which would be worse.

Satin & Thorne (Silk & Thorne 2)

Printed in Great Britain
by Amazon

52259056R00064